This book belongs to:

....

Sometimes Mimi and her friends fly all the way to our huge
world and have lots of fun tiptoeing into toyshops and playing
hide-and-seek in the dolls' houses. Before they fly home again,
they whisper their stories to Clare and Cally,
so now YOU can hear them too!

For YOU, the readers of this book. May you always be LUCKY! - C.B.
For Julie, Geoff, Jenna and Calvin, with lots of love xx - C.J-I.

Hazel   Rose   Mimi   Acorn   Lily

First published 2017 by Macmillan Children's Books
an imprint of Pan Macmillan,
20 New Wharf Road, London N1 9RR
Associated companies throughout the world

www.panmacmillan.com

ISBN: 978-1-5098-1908-9
Text copyright © Clare Bevan 2017
Illustrations copyright © Cally Johnson-Isaacs 2017

1 3 5 7 9 8 6 4 2

A CIP catalogue record for this book is available from the British Library.

Printed in China

mimi's magical Fairy Friends

Lucky the Fairy Rabbit

by Clare Bevan and Cally Johnson-Isaacs

MACMILLAN CHILDREN'S BOOKS

One morning, Mimi flew across the garden and said, "Let's have a sports day!"
"Hooray!" cried Acorn. "We can loop and swoop and hover and bounce."
"We can all win a silver star," said Hazel.

But Lily was gazing at something stripy and strange.
It was flapping and floating down, down and landing on the grass . . .

"It's a flying carpet," shouted Lily. "But why is it here?"
"We could sit on it and find out," said Hazel.

As soon as everyone was comfy, the carpet began to ripple and twitch.
"It wants to fly away!" gasped Rose. "Where will it take us?"
"Let's make a wish," said Mimi.

The fairies closed their eyes and sang:

"Wonderful carpet, whirl us away
To a sandy beach on a sunshiny day."

The carpet jiggled, the fairies giggled — and they flip-flapped over the hills.

Soon they landed at the seaside!
The waves splashed and the sand glittered in the sunshine.
It was the perfect place for a fairy sports day.

Mimi did the loveliest loop,

Rose was the fastest flyer,

Acorn won the swirliest swoop and Hazel managed the highest hover.

Lily was the only fairy who hadn't won a silver star.
"Never mind," said Mimi kindly. "Perhaps you'll win at the
biggest bounce."
Lily tried REALLY hard. She did her best bounces ever,
but they just weren't big enough.

Meanwhile someone behind her was bouncing brilliantly.
BOING! BOING!

"Oh dear," puffed Lily. "I think I'll build a sandcastle instead." While she was digging, she whispered a wish:

"I didn't win a sports day prize,
So I wish for luck and a small surprise."

Lily put down her spade and listened. BOING! BOING!
Someone was watching her – someone very bouncy indeed!

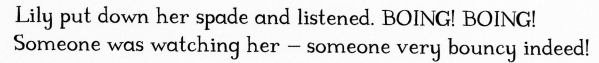

"Hello, little rabbit!" laughed Lily.
"Would you like to help me?"

The rabbit dug heaps of sand while
Lily smoothed and shaped the walls.
Then they both bounced away to
find shells and pebbles and bits of
wood.

Soon their castle had doors and windows and a tiny drawbridge.
It looked beautiful!

"Thank you, bouncy rabbit," said Lily with a yawn.
She waved at him as he hopped away — and a moment
later she was fast asleep.

Lily had a wonderful dream that she was inside her beautiful castle.
All the walls were golden and all the pictures shone.
She felt like a fairy princess as she skipped up the twisty stairs.

A river was swirling around the castle walls, and her rabbit sailed
by in a little bouncy boat.
"Wait for me!" yelled Lily.
Then a real watery wave tickled her toes and she woke up.

As Lily opened her eyes, she saw the little rabbit.

He wasn't bouncing. Or digging.
He was bobbing around the sandcastle on a glass bottle!

Lily jumped up and rescued her rabbit from the sea.
Then she looked at the bottle. When she shook it, it rattled.
And when she opened it, out fell a tiny flute and a mermaid's message:

Find my treasures,
my crown and
my comb.
Then play my flute
to call me home.

"How can we find the treasures?" wondered Lily.
The sea was creeping closer and the beach was growing smaller.

The other fairies came fluttering down.
When they saw the letter, everyone wanted to help.

They looped,

they swooped,

they hovered.

But no one spotted a single shiny pearl.
They were about to give up when the rabbit
hopped up a sandy hill and began to BOING!

The fairies flew up the hill – but all they saw was a twist of string.
"That's not a treasure," said Rose.

Lily stroked the little rabbit.
"Why are you bouncing?" she murmured as she tugged the string.
It was salty and slippery and it seemed to be stuck!

Now everyone wanted to play Tug the String, and soon there was a long line of fairies and pets all pulling as hard as they could until . . .

POP!

They all tumbled down and out came a tangle of knots, some slimy seaweed, an old fishing net and . . .

the mermaid's treasure!
Everyone clapped and cheered as Lily untangled the strings.

She found a sea-blue crown,

a sparkly comb,

a glittering mirror and
a necklace of pearls.

"Well done, bouncy rabbit!" said Mimi.
"Now Lily can play the mermaid's flute."

Lily took a deep breath and blew. She had never played a flute
before, but a magical tune trilled and floated across the foamy sea.

"Look!" cried all the fairies at once.
The Mermaid Queen was riding towards them on her royal dolphin.
When Lily gave her the treasures, the mermaid thanked her and sang:

"Now you see how lucky you are –
You've won a pet and a silver star!"

Then SWISH! She twisted away and vanished below the waves.
Lily paddled happily back to her friends holding a starfish
made of shiny silver!

"But you are the best treasure of all," she told her rabbit
as they hopped onto the magic carpet . . .

"I think I shall call you LUCKY!" she said with a big smile.

Your very own Lucky and Lily!

Push the tab into the rabbit's tummy.

Hold the fairy so her back is facing you. Squeeze her legs inwards and insert the tab marked with a star into the slot underneath her foot.

Now you have your very own fairy friends to play with!

Look out for more characters in the series!